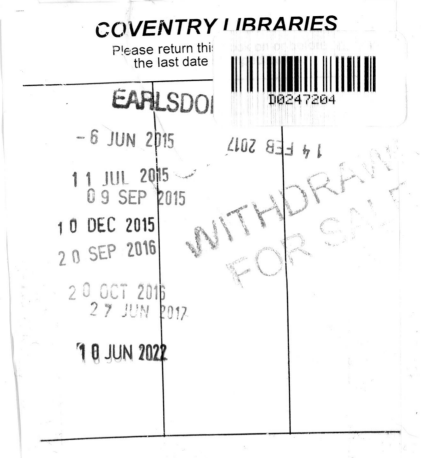
as a Rainbow Magic special. This version has
been specially adapted for developing readers
in conjunction with a Reading Consultant.

Coventry City Council	
CEN*	
3 8002 02210 844 5	
Askews & Holts	Mar-2015
SHORT CHAPTER	£4.99

Reading Consultant: Prue Goodwin, lecturer in literacy and children's books.

ORCHARD BOOKS
338 Euston Road, London NW1 3BH
Orchard Books Australia
Level 17/207 Kent Street, Sydney, NSW 2000

This text first published in 2009 by Orchard Books
This Early Reader edition published in 2015
© 2015 Rainbow Magic Limited.
A HIT Entertainment company. Rainbow Magic
is a trademark of Rainbow Magic Limited.
Reg. U.S. Pat. & Tm. Off. And other countries.

HiT entertainment

Illustrations © Orchard Books 2015

A CIP catalogue record for this book is available
from the British Library.

ISBN 978 1 40833 631 1
1 3 5 7 9 10 8 6 4 2

Printed in China

Orchard Books is a division of Hachette Children's Books,
an Hachette UK company

www.hachette.co.uk

Keira
the Film Star Fairy

by Daisy Meadows

ORCHARD

www.rainbowmagic.co.uk

Jack Frost's
Ice Castle

The Woods

Gardens

Glade

Cottage

Contents

Story One

The Silver Script

The Silver Script

"Look, there's Julianna Stewart!" whispered Kirsty Tate, spying the film star reading her script.

"Who would have thought a famous actress would come here to Wetherbury Village?" said her best friend, Rachel Walker.

9

Julianna Stewart was starring in a movie called *The Starlight Chronicles*, and it was being filmed in Mrs Croft's garden! Someone from a film company had knocked on her door one day and asked if they could use her pretty cottage for the movie.

Mrs Croft was a friend of Kirsty's parents and had managed to get the girls parts as magical fairies – which was perfect for them! They had secretly visited Fairyland many

times and were always ready
to protect their fluttery friends
from mean Jack Frost and his
naughty goblin servants.

"I can't wait to try on our costumes!" grinned Kirsty.

 The film set bustled with people. Helpers known as runners fetched props, and dancers practised their steps. The girls watched as Julianna took her place in front of Chad Stenning, the actor playing the fairy prince.

"And . . . action!" cried the director.

Everyone watched as Chad gave a deep bow. "Please walk with me on the terrace. There is something I must say." He offered his arm to Julianna and led her off the set.

"Excellent!" announced the director.

"I haven't seen that runner before," said Rachel, nudging her friend. "He seems in a terrible hurry."

The runner rushed past the actors, then snatched a script from the director's table.

"That's not a runner," Kirsty said breathessly, spotting a patch of green skin. "It's a goblin!"

Rachel gasped as she caught sight of a pair of warty green feet.

The girls started to follow

him just as the director called,
"Action!"

Everyone waited for Julianna
and Chad to start speaking.
But they were totally silent.

At last Julianna spoke.

"My mind's gone blank!" she
exclaimed.

"That's strange," whispered
Rachel. "She's never forgotten
her words before. Something
– or someone – is upsetting
things."

"We must find that goblin!"
Kirsty replied.

Rachel led the way along a path of stepping stones that led to a meadow behind Mrs Croft's cottage. It was full of mobile homes in all shapes and sizes. The actors and crew were staying here together during filming.

"That way!" cried Rachel, watching the goblin's baseball cap disappearing behind a plush-looking silver trailer.

Suddenly, a wardrobe mistress with a tape measure around her neck pushed a rail of fancy fairy outfits right across their path.

"Coming through!" she cried.

Kirsty sighed. "We'll never catch the goblin now. It'll be too late by the time we get past these costumes."

As the girls tried to step around the rail, tiny scarlet stars began to shimmer and fizz above a beautiful gown until suddenly, a pretty fairy burst out from it, landing on the rail.

"Hi!" she smiled. "I'm Keira the Film Star Fairy."

"Hello!" grinned Kirsty and Rachel, following the fairy as she fluttered to a quiet part of the meadow.

"I look after movie-makers in Fairyland and the human world," she explained. "And I really need your help."

Kirsty and Rachel listened as Keira told them about her three precious magical objects.

"The silver script makes sure the actors get their lines right. The magical megaphone helps directors organise everyone and the enchanted clapperboard gets the camera rolling. Everything was fine," she sighed, "until Jack Frost decided he wanted to be a film star."

Keira told the girls how the Ice Lord had sent his goblins to snatch the silver script.

"If we don't find it," the little fairy went on, "Julianna and the others won't be able to perform properly!"

"We just saw a goblin steal a script!" cried Kirsty, as Keira fluttered into her jacket pocket.

"This way!" said the fairy, pointing her shimmering wand towards the woods.

Kirsty peeped through the trees. "I can see the goblin!" she gasped. "He's got the silver script, and he's not alone!"

"I have to be the director!" they heard a pointy-nosed goblin shout.

"Only if I can be the prince," snapped another.

Within moments they were tugging at the script and arguing.

"I've got an idea," whispered Rachel. "Keira, would you be able to magic us some smart clothes?"

"Of course!" replied Keira, waving her wand and transforming their outfits into suits and dark glasses.

The girls stepped into the clearing.

"We're from Hollywood," Rachel announced. "And we thought you might like some tips."

A goblin with big ears shrugged his shoulders.

"Let's start with some acting exercises," began Rachel. "I'll give you a scene to act out."

"Shan't," yelled the goblin clutching the silver script.

"Oh," sighed Rachel. "But you've got the starring role!"

"I'll do it!" he cried suddenly.

"Just imagine," continued Rachel, "that you are a famous author. Now pretend you are coming to my office to deliver your new story."

"Are we ready?" cut in Kirsty suddenly. "Then . . . action!"

The goblin opened an imaginary door.

"I think you'll enjoy reading this," he began importantly, handing her the silver script.

Suddenly, Keira burst from Kirsty's pocket and tapped the silver script with her wand, shrinking it to fairy size.

"Thanks, Mr Goblin Writer!" she smiled.

The goblins squawked and leapt with rage.

"This is going back to Fairyland," she told them

firmly. "Where it belongs."

When the silly goblins had run off to hide from Jack Frost, Keira smiled.

"Thank you," she said, magically changing the girls back into their normal clothes, and disappearing in a puff of fairy dust.

"Goodbye!" waved the girls.

"Let's go back to the film set," Kirsty suggested, linking arms with her best friend. "I'll bet those rehearsals are on track again!"

Story Two

The Magical Megaphone

The Magical
Megaphone

Back in Mrs Croft's garden,
people scurried around
everywhere. "Let's sit over
there," suggested Rachel,
pointing to a wooden bench. It
was the perfect place to watch
the rehearsal.

"Let's roll!" announced the director.

Everyone waited for Julianna to say her first line, but instead, she wandered over to Chad, who was still having his make-up done!

"Miss Stewart," began the director gently. "The scene with your fairy servants under the

disappeared.

"What a gormless bunch!" barked Jack Frost, storming up and down the courtyard. "Can't you lot do anything I tell you?"

"What's up with him?"
sniffed one of the goblins,
nudging a pal in the ribs.
The other goblin gawped at
his master then pulled a silly
face. "Lucky we've got these

earplugs in!" he sniggered.

"Time to go!" beamed Keira, pointing her wand at the girls and holding on tight to her magical megaphone. In a fizz of stars, she whisked them all away with Jack Frost's shouts still echoing in the distance.

After everyone had said goodbye, a sparkling shower of magic from Keira's wand turned Rachel and Kirsty back to human size again. Could this holiday get any more exciting?

Story Three

The Enchanted Clapperboard

The Enchanted Clapperboard

Kirsty and Rachel were both feeling very excited. It was finally time for them to play their parts as extras in *The Starlight Chronicles*! "I can't wait to show our costumes to Keira," whispered Kirsty.

Each girl was dressed in a pale pink gown, and with all the other extras, had spent the morning having their hair and make-up done. The first scene was to be filmed inside Mrs Croft's pretty house. They would be attending the fairy princess on the morning of her wedding.

"I hope I can remember where to stand!" said an extra called Angel. Her friend, Emily, anxiously bent down to tie the ribbons on her satin slippers.

Suddenly, the door opened and there were gasps as Julianna stepped onto the set.

"You look perfect!" exclaimed Rachel.

Large dazzling spotlights shone onto the sparkling set as the director held up his special movie clapperboard.

"Quiet please," he began. "Lights, camera . . ."

The girls waited to hear the word "action", but nothing happened.

"The clapperboard is stuck," he said, frowning.

The flustered crew tried to get it working, but it refused to snap shut. An assistant ran up and passed the director two thick wooden sticks he had found in the props department.

"My camera won't work, either," said a confused camera operator.

"There's something funny going on around here," whispered Rachel.

"Look," Kirsty said quietly to her friend, pointing. "That camera's glowing!"

The girls stared as Keira whooshed out of the lens.

"Oh girls," she cried. "Jack Frost has stolen my enchanted clapperboard, and given it to his goblins!"

Rachel and Kirsty were horrified. "What does it do?" asked Rachel.

"It makes sure filming always goes to plan," Keira explained.

"That must be why it's going wrong today," guessed Kirsty.

Suddenly there was a giggle outside the door, and the sound of footsteps on the stairs.

"That sounded like a goblin," said Kirsty. "Do you think the enchanted clapperboard is here?"

"If you were fairies," said Keira, "it would be much easier to search around without being seen."

Keira waved her wand and a cascade of golden fairy dust

magically shrank them to
fairy size.

"Let's go!" said Kirsty,
swooping upstairs and
following the sound of giggling
into Mrs Croft's bedroom. Two
goblins were bouncing up and
down on the bed. One had a
clapperboard under his arm.

"That's the enchanted clapperboard!" said Keira.

"Give that back to Keira right now!" declared Rachel, fluttering forward.

The goblin was so surprised, he lost his balance and bounced off the bed with a loud crash. Then, without looking back, they both shot out of the door, still clutching the enchanted clapperboard.

At the top of the stairs, the goblins played tug-of-war with it, until suddenly one of them lost their balance and they both tumbled all the way down.

"Come on!" Keira cried, zooming after the goblins. "We have to stop them!"

Downstairs, a sound technician had wedged her microphone in the old ceiling beams and three runners were trying to pull it free. Half the costumes had gone missing,

and the make-up artist's
brushes had fallen through the
floorboards. The poor director
was sitting in the middle of it
all with his head in his hands.

"We have to finish filming
tonight," he muttered.
"Mrs Croft is coming back

tomorrow! Let's set up a screen and watch the rushes," he went on.

"What are the rushes?" asked Rachel as everyone sprang into action.

"They're the scenes from the day before," Keira explained. "The director always checks them to make sure nothing needs to be re-shot."

The girls watched as two runners pointed a projector at the white wall, drew the curtains and turned off the

lights. The room was soon
packed as everyone gathered
for the viewing.

Through the gloom, Kirsty
saw something move behind
the sofa.

The goblins were watching
the film scenes and scowling.
"I'd make a much better star,"

one said, tucking the enchanted clapperboard under his arm and jumping in front of the projector screen.

"No you wouldn't," squeaked the other one. "I would!"

Everyone in the room gasped.

"Quick – grab it!" cried Keira.

The three fluttering fairies reached the enchanted clapperboard a second too late.

"I don't remember filming this," said the director, frowning. The goblins began pushing

each other as the outlines of
their bodies filled the white
wall behind them.

"Who hired these naughty
extras?" he demanded. "And
where did they get those
hideous costumes?"

As the goblins shoved
and fought, the enchanted
clapperboard fell to the ground.

"This is our chance!" said Rachel. As a runner jumped up to chase the goblins from the room, the three friends zipped towards the clapperboard. The film crew were so busy staring at the goblins, no one saw the little fairy land beside the enchanted clapperboard and shrink it back to fairy size.

"I've got it!" she cried, as

the three of them swooped out through the open window.

Just then, they heard Mrs Croft's front door open, and the goblins ran out scowling, and disappeared into the woods.

"Thanks for your help today," said Keira. "Now

filming can get back to normal."

With a swoop of her magic wand, she returned Kirsty and Rachel to their normal size.

"I'm going to take the enchanted clapperboard back to Fairyland," explained

Keira. "But I've got a feeling that *The Starlight Chronicles* is going to be a

sparkling success!"

With that, she disappeared in a burst of golden light.

"We're ready for you now, girls!" a runner called to them. "The cameras are working again."

Kirsty and Rachel hurried inside, just in time to hear the director say three truly magical words:

"Lights! Camera! Action!"

**If you enjoyed this story,
you may want to read**

Tamara the Tooth Fairy
Early Reader

Here's how the story begins...

"My wobbly tooth has finally fallen out!" Kirsty Tate called out to her best friend. She had arrived just that morning at Rachel Walker's house, where she was staying for part of the summer holidays.

"That's brilliant! We've never met the Tooth Fairy!" said

Rachel, as the girls changed into their pyjamas. "I wonder what she's like?"

Climbing into bed, Kirsty put her tooth safely under the pillow. "The Tooth Fairy is so quiet that she never wakes children up," Kirsty yawned.

The two friends had a very special secret. They had often visited Fairyland. Sometimes naughty Jack Frost and his goblins made terrible mischief, and the girls had often helped the fairies defeat them. Rachel smiled and turned out the light. It had been a long day, and the girls were soon asleep.

When Rachel's alarm clock went off in the morning, she sat up and looked eagerly over to where her best friend was sleeping.

Kirsty opened her eyes and lifted her pillow. "My tooth is still here," she said in a disappointed voice.

"The Tooth Fairy is probably confused because you're staying here instead of at home,"

Rachel said, jumping out of bed to comfort her friend. "I expect she'll come tonight."

"Perhaps she left a coin and forgot to take the tooth," said Kirsty, picking up the pillow and shaking it. "Or maybe the coin got stuck inside somehow?"

Read
Tamara the Tooth Fairy
Early Reader
to find out
what happens next!

EARLY READER

RAINBOW magic™

Shannon the Ocean Fairy

Summer the Holiday Fairy

Florence the Friendship Fairy

Belle the Birthday Fairy

Kylie the Carnival Fairy

Flora the Fancy Dress Fairy

Mia the Bridesmaid Fairy

Selena the Sleepover Fairy

Destiny the Pop Star Fairy

Start reading with the Rainbow Magic fairies

Meet the first seven
Rainbow Magic Fairies

Ruby the Red Fairy

Amber the Orange Fairy

Saffron the Yellow Fairy

Fern the Green Fairy

Sky the Blue Fairy

Izzy the Indigo Fairy

Heather the Violet Fairy

There's a fairy book for everyone at:
www.rainbowmagicbooks.co.uk

RAINBOW magic

Become a
Rainbow Magic
fairy friend and be the first to
see sneak peeks of new books.

There are lots of special offers and exclusive
competitions to win sparkly
Rainbow Magic prizes.

Sign up today at
www.rainbowmagicbooks.co.uk